The Wildlife ABC & 123

A Nature Alphabet & Counting Book

Jan Thornhill

MAPLE
TREE
PRESS

Maple Tree Press Inc.
51 Front Street East, Suite 200, Toronto, Ontario M5E 1B3
www.mapletreepress.com

Distributed in Canada by Raincoast Books
9050 Shaughnessy Street, Vancouver, British Columbia V6P 6E5

Distributed in the United States by Publishers Group West
1700 Fourth Street, Berkeley, California 94710

We acknowledge the financial support of the Canada Council
for the Arts, the Ontario Arts Council, the Government of
Canada through the Book Publishing Industry Development
Program (BPIDP), and the Government of Ontario through the Ontario Media
Development Corporation's Book Initiative for our publishing activities.

ONTARIO ARTS COUNCIL
CONSEIL DES ARTS DE L'ONTARIO

Cataloguing in Publication Data

Thornhill, Jan
    The Wildlife ABC & 123 : a nature alphabet & counting book / Jan Thornhill.

A combination of the author's previously published titles: The Wildlife ABC and The
Wildlife 123. ISBN 1-897066-09-0

    1. English language—Alphabet—Juvenile literature. 2. Counting—Juvenile literature.
    3. Animals—Pictorial works—Juvenile literature.

    I. Title. II. Title: Wildlife ABC and 123.

        QL49.T563 2004   j590   C2004-900976-1

Design & art direction: Wycliffe Smith and Claudia Dávila
Illustrations: Jan Thornhill

Printed in Hong Kong

A   B   C   D   E   F

The Wildlife ABC

Aa

A is for Auk
Who lives by the sea,

Bb

B is for Beaver
Felling a tree.

Cc

C is for Caterpillar
Who eats a lot,

Dd

D is for Dragonfly
Flitting by when it's hot.

Ee

E is for Eagle
Seeking salmon to eat,

Ff

F is for Frog
With webbed hind feet.

Gg

G is for Goose
Paddling under a bridge,

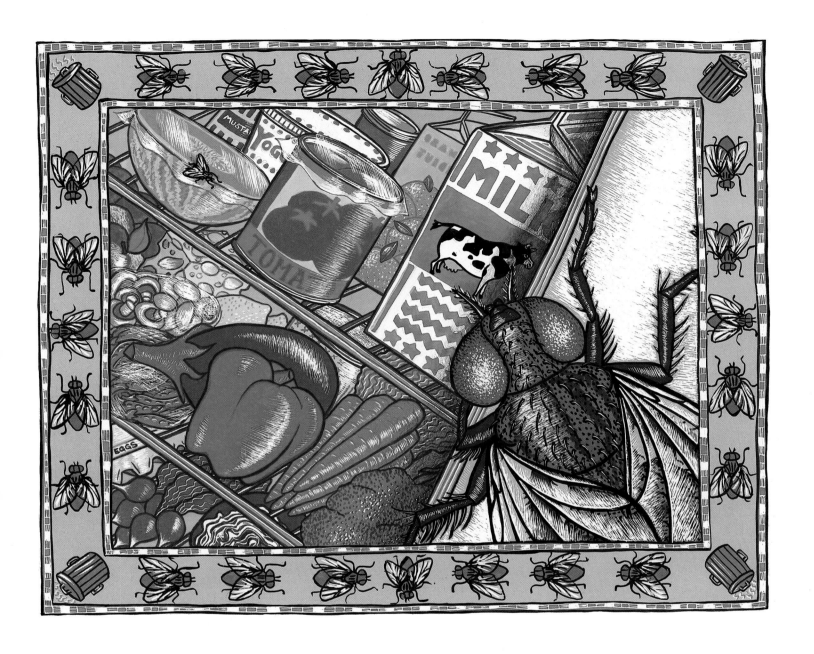

Hh

H is for Housefly
Inspecting your fridge.

Ii

I is for Inchworm
Sneaking along the ground,

Jj

J is for Jumping Mouse
Hopping around.

Kk

K is for Killer Whale
In the deep blue sea,

Ll

L is for Loon
Who swims excellently.

Mm

M is for Moose
Munching plants in a park,

Nn

N is for Nighthawk
Catching bugs in the dark.

Oo

O is for Otter
Look at him go!

Pp

P is for Polar Bear
Walking on snow.

Qq

Q is for Queen Bee
Laying eggs to hatch,

Rr

R is for Raccoon
See her lifting the latch?

Ss

S is for Salmon
Swimming up a creek,

Tt

T is for Turtle
Her mouth is a beak.

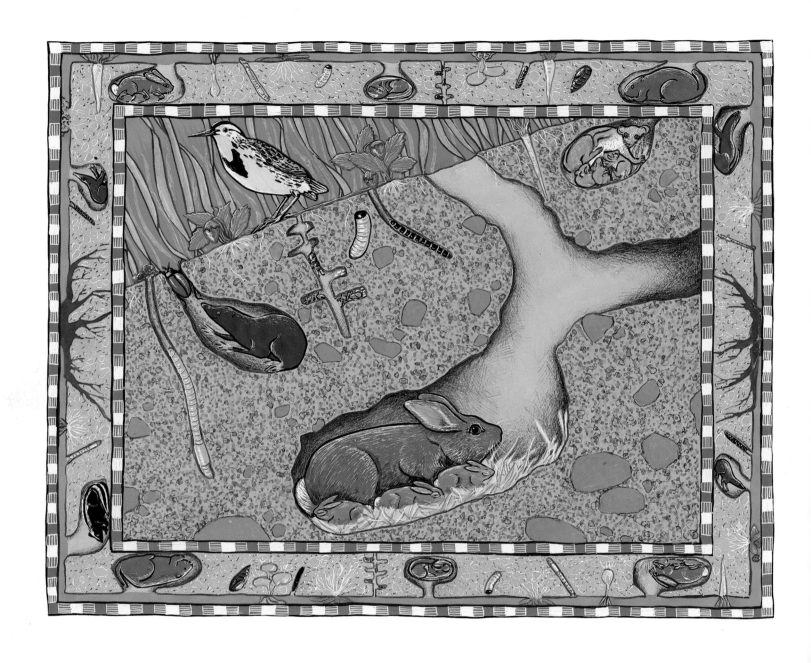

Uu

U is for Underground
Who lives there?

Vv

V is for Vole
Who had better beware!

Ww

W is for Whooping Crane
Wading near shore,

Xx

X is for X-ray
Of a big dinosaur.

Yy

Y is for Yellowjacket
Who might live near you,

Zz

And Z is for Zoo!
Can you tell who's who?

Zz

Zoo *(border repeats animals A-Z)*

1. Ruby-Throated Hummingbird
2. Brown Bat
3. Zebra Butterfly
4. American Redstart
5. Chickadee
6. Grizzly Bear
7. Magpie
8. Walrus
9. Groundhog
10. White-Tailed Deer
11. Mountain Goat
12. Pronghorn Antelope
13. Caribou
14. Muskox
15. Pileated Woodpecker
16. Wolf
17. Bighorn Sheep
18. Bobcat
19. Porcupine
20. Skunk
21. Barn Owl
22. Opossum with young
23. Hare
24. Badger
25. Massasauga Rattler
26. Toad
27. Box Turtle
28. Wood Duck
29. Yellow Perch
30. Brook Trout
31. Painted Turtle
32. Lake Sturgeon
33. Crayfish

The Wildlife 123

1

One Panda

2

Two Giraffes

3

Three Starfish

4

Four Parrots

5

Five Tigers

6

Six Crocodiles

7

Seven Monkeys

8

Eight Camels

9

Nine Sparrows

10

Ten Mountain Goats

11

Eleven Elephants

12

Twelve Ants

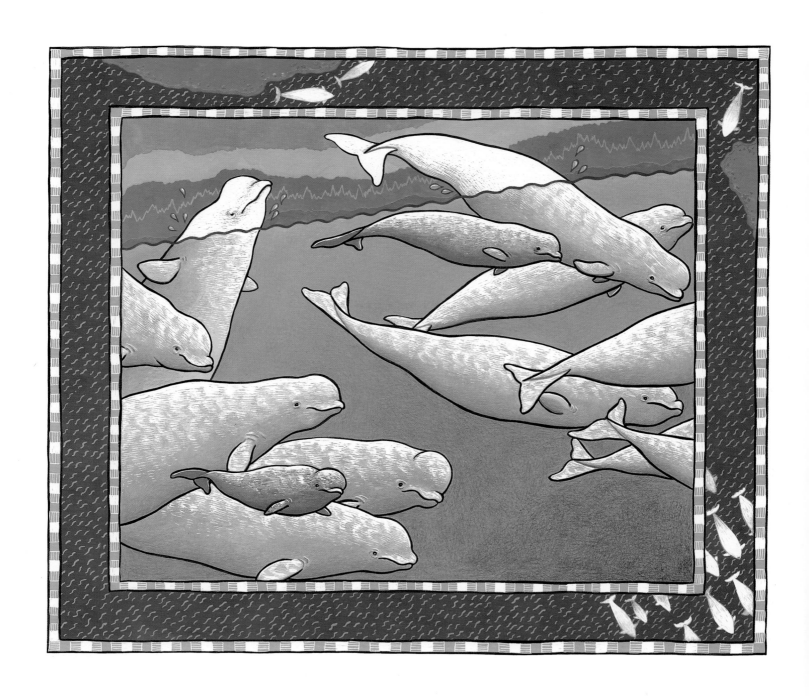

13

Thirteen Whales

14

Fourteen Lemurs

15

Fifteen Kangaroos

16

Sixteen Crabs

17

Seventeen Tortoises

18

Eighteen Prairie Dogs

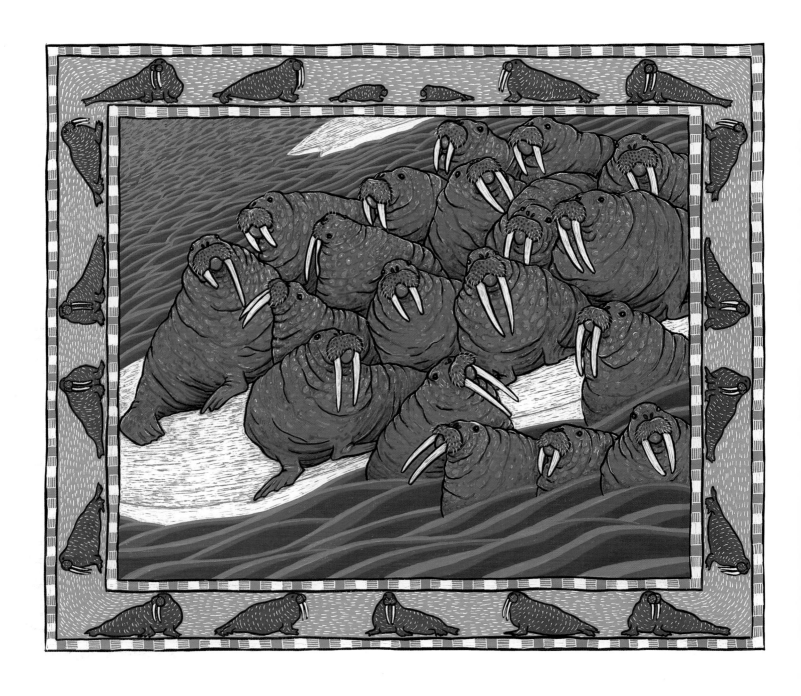

19

Nineteen Walruses

20

Twenty Tropical Fish

25

Twenty-five Butterflies

50

Fifty Flamingos

100

One Hundred Penguins

1000

One Thousand Tadpoles

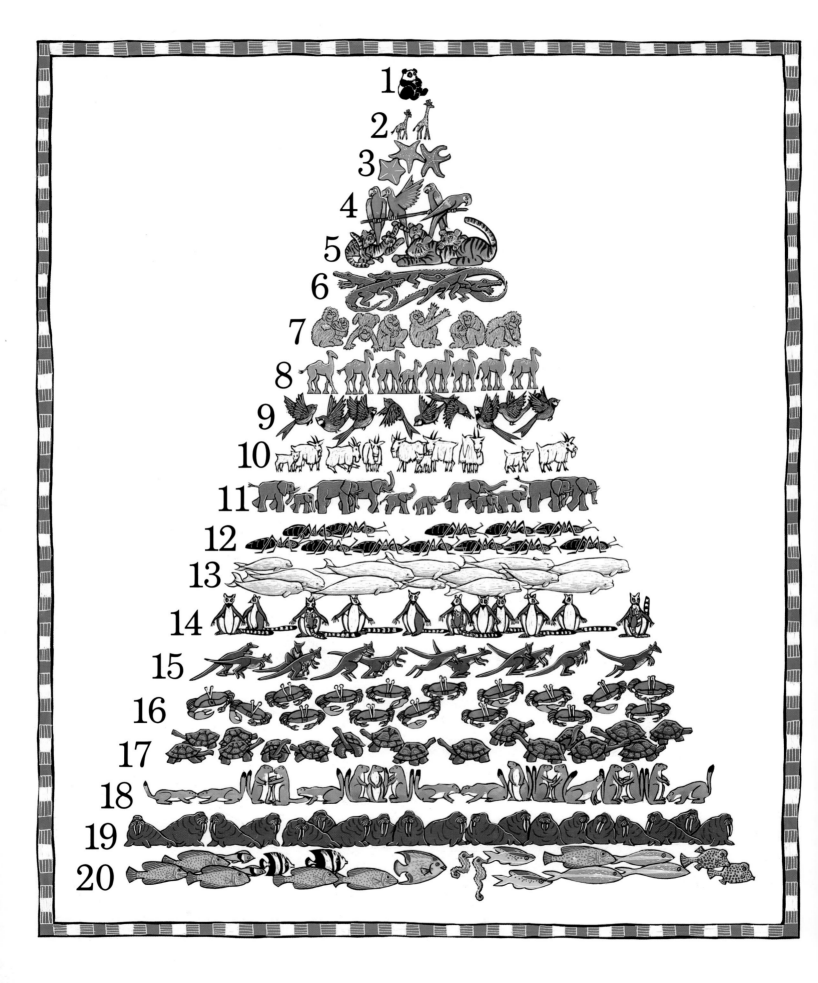

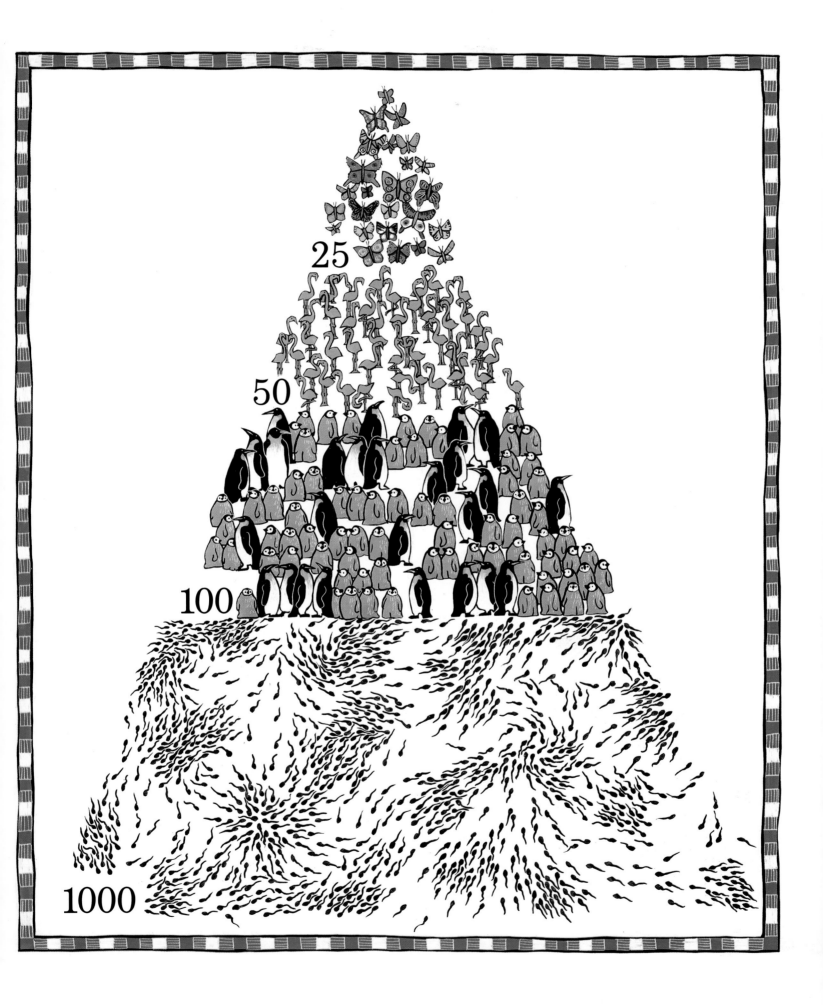

25

50

100

1000

The Wildlife 123

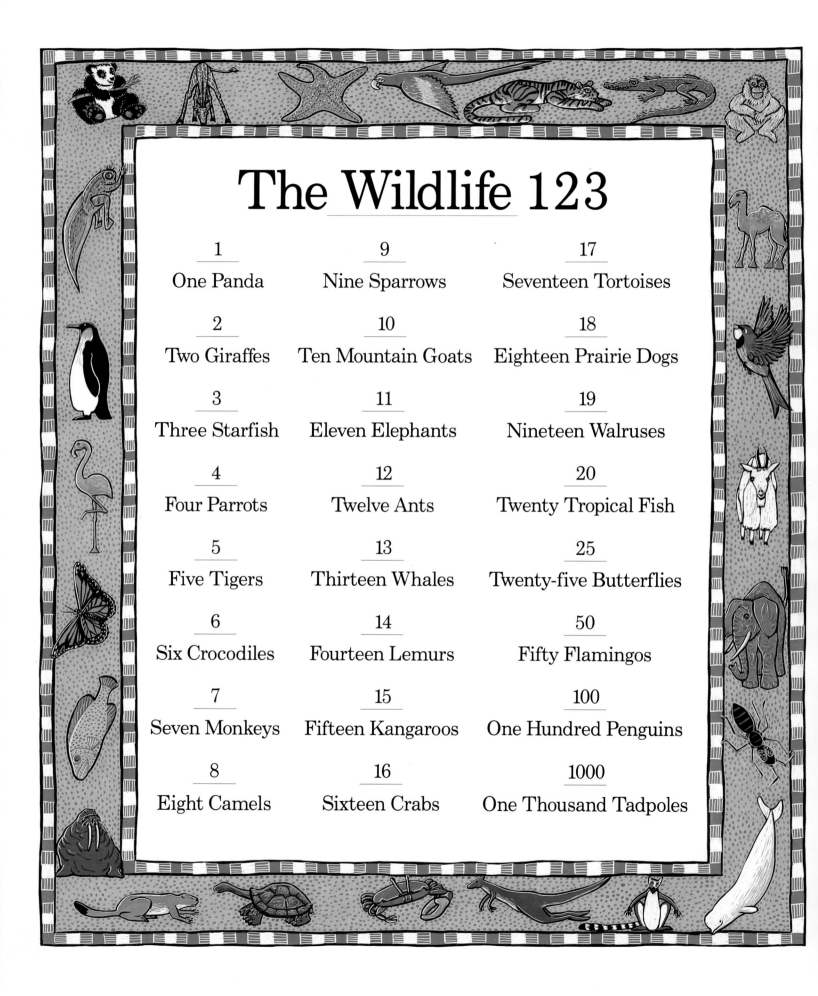

1	9	17
One Panda	Nine Sparrows	Seventeen Tortoises
2	10	18
Two Giraffes	Ten Mountain Goats	Eighteen Prairie Dogs
3	11	19
Three Starfish	Eleven Elephants	Nineteen Walruses
4	12	20
Four Parrots	Twelve Ants	Twenty Tropical Fish
5	13	25
Five Tigers	Thirteen Whales	Twenty-five Butterflies
6	14	50
Six Crocodiles	Fourteen Lemurs	Fifty Flamingos
7	15	100
Seven Monkeys	Fifteen Kangaroos	One Hundred Penguins
8	16	1000
Eight Camels	Sixteen Crabs	One Thousand Tadpoles

Nature Notes

ABC Nature Notes

Aa
Great Auk
with a colony of gannets

Although there are several smaller species of auk still found in the North Atlantic, the great auk is now extinct because of over-hunting. These large, flightless birds were easy prey out of the water and their eggs were collected for food. The last known pair was killed in 1844. Beside them was found a single broken egg.

Bb
Beaver
with a woolly caterpillar, swimming beaver, great blue heron

The beaver, which is the second largest rodent in the world, has chisel-like, self-sharpening teeth that it uses to cut down trees, remove branches, and strip off bark. After they eat the bark, beavers build dams and lodges with the stripped trees. A beaver's flat tail acts as a rudder in water, helps the beaver balance upright while felling trees, and is slapped loudly on the water's surface to warn the family when danger threatens.

Cc
Black Swallowtail Caterpillar
with eggs, chrysalis, adult butterfly

Caterpillars hatch from eggs laid by butterflies and moths. In this, the second of its four life stages, the insect devours large quantities of plant matter. Because the black swallowtail caterpillar prefers plants such as cultivated carrots, parsley, celery, and dill, it is often found in backyard gardens. Over several weeks of intense feeding, the caterpillar increases greatly in size before pupating into a chrysalis.

There the adult develops, emerging finally as a butterfly.

Dd
Dragonfly
with mergansers and pickerelweed

Dragonflies, with their large eyes, moveable heads, and ability to fly both forward and backward, catch huge numbers of mosquitoes and other flying insects. Their eggs, usually deposited on the water, hatch into naiads, the dragonfly's larvae. After several years of eating other aquatic creatures, the naiad crawls out of the water and the fully formed adult emerges from a slit in its back.

Ee
Bald Eagle
with eaglets in nest, humpback whales breaching, sea lions basking

Bald eagles, who mate for life, build huge nests (some weigh two tons) in tall trees. The young eaglets are fed fish, which their parents catch with their long, curved claws. After the eaglets grow their first dark brown feathers, they learn to fly by exercising on the wide platform of their nest. The bald eagle has been an endangered species in many areas because much of the forest in which they find nesting trees has been cut down for lumber or development.

Ff
Leopard Frog
with a ladybug, ant, white admiral butterfly

The leopard frog begins its life underwater as one of a mass of jelly-protected eggs. It hatches into a tiny tadpole, which breathes through gills like a fish. Eventually, legs and lungs develop and soon after the tail is reabsorbed into the body to feed the final metamorphosis of tadpole into frog, who can leave the water to breathe on land. The leopard frog has long, muscular hind legs for hopping, and webbed feet for swimming, so that it can escape predators both on land and in the water.

Gg
Canada Goose
with a black squirrel and cardinal

The unmistakable honks of Canada geese ringing across the sky as they migrate in V formation inspired the Cree Indians to call them "hounds of heaven." In the spring, while the goose sits on her two to nine eggs, her mate for life (the gander) stays close by on guard. When the hatchlings appear, both parents stand near so the goslings will recognize them in the future and, because the young identify with the first creature they see, will realize that they too are geese. In the following weeks, the downy yellow brood, which can leave the nest right away, will learn by imitating their parents.

Hh
Housefly
in its common habitat

Because they can easily adapt to different environments, houseflies are found all over the world. Their large, curved, compound eyes are made up of about 4,000 hexagonal lenses, each of which points in a slightly different direction so that each sees only part of an object. This confusion of images is joined together in the fly's brain, making one coherent picture. The housefly's two single wings, which distinguish it from other flying insects, can beat 200 times a second.

Ii
Inchworm
with a monarch butterfly, nuthatch, and asters, milkweed, burdock, plantain, goldenrod, dock

Inchworms, also known as measuring worms or loopers, are the larvae of one of the largest families of moths. Their unique way of moving developed because of their lack of legs in the middle segments of their bodies. Some inchworms resemble twigs when they grip a branch with their hind legs and let their long bodies project out on an angle. If they keep perfectly still, this trick of mimicry can fool predators.

Jj
Woodland Jumping Mouse
with a moth and owl

The woodland jumping mouse has large hind legs and a tail longer than its body to help it balance when leaping about—sometimes 2 m (6 ft.) in a single bound. Good swimmers, woodland jumping mice live in burrows close to water, eating seeds, berries, and insects. They are most active at night, when they must be wary of owls, one of their major predators.

Kk
Killer Whale
with herring gulls

The highly intelligent killer whales, some 8 m (25 ft.) long and weighing six tons, travel in pods of three to fifty animals—although about ten is the most common number. These tight-knit family groups can be told apart by the different noises, calls, and piercing sounds they make. They eat mostly cod, herring, and salmon, but will also hunt sea birds or seals, and on occasion will even attack other whales.

Ll
Loon
with lake trout and yellow perch

On clear northern lakes in the summer, the cackling, yodeling, and haunting wails of the loon are a familiar sound. Such specialized diving birds that they cannot walk properly on land, loons are very fast and agile underwater, capable of traveling several hundred metres (feet) before surfacing for air. Their diet consists mainly of fish, but they also eat leeches, crayfish, and frogs. Although loon chicks can dive within a day of hatching, they are fed by their parents for several months. If danger threatens, the chicks are carried away on a parent's back or tucked under a wing.

Mm
Moose
with diving kingfisher, flicker on tree trunk, dragonfly

In the summer, moose are often seen feeding on underwater and floating plants such as pond lilies. Excellent swimmers and divers, it is not unusual for them to stay submerged for a full minute or to swim across a wide lake. The distinctive antlers of the males, which can span 2 m (6 ft.), grow anew each year. After shedding the velvety skin that feeds their growth, the antlers fall off in the fall, and a new set begins growing in by the spring.

Nn

Nighthawk
with bats, luna moth

Nighthawks, which are not true hawks, are most often seen at twilight and after dark, flitting high above city buildings or over open fields. Flying with their huge mouths agape, they can capture large numbers of mosquitoes in a single snap or snatch up a large moth. Nighthawks have adapted easily to city life, laying their eggs on gravel-covered roofs, perfect camouflage for the mottled coloring of the shells.

Oo

River Otter
with rose-breasted grosbeaks, white-tailed deer, two otters in the river

River otters, long and streamlined with webbed feet and waterproof fur, are wonderful swimmers, spending much of their time in water frolicking and catching fish. They are playful all their lives, and enjoy slipping down mudslides in the summer and sliding down snowbanks in the winter. Two cubs are born each spring in a riverbank tunnel. The cubs stay with their mother a long time, learning from her the skills they will need to survive on their own.

Pp

Polar Bear
with cubs, Arctic hare, snowy owl

In the fall, the female polar bear digs a snug den in a snowdrift. There she gives birth to two cubs weighing barely 0.5 kg (1 lb.) each. In the early spring, when the cubs have grown to about 12 kg (25 lb.), the mother brings them outside. They will stay with her for two years, traveling great distances across the Arctic landscape, learning to hunt seals for themselves.

Qq

Queen Honeybees
with attendant workers

Although there may be several thousand worker bees and several hundred male drones in a hive, there is only one queen. Attended by workers, the queen can lay 1,000 eggs a day. When the eggs hatch, some of the larvae are chosen to become queens and are fed a special diet of "royal jelly" instead of the worker mixture of pollen and honey. In the late spring, the reigning queen leaves the hive with a swarm of workers to found a new colony. Soon after her departure, the first young queen to emerge takes the old queen's place.

Rr

Raccoon
with young

The raccoon roams at night and is an omnivore, meaning it will eat almost anything. In the wild its favorite foods are crayfish, bird and turtle eggs, freshwater clams, nuts, and seeds. The young, born in the spring, spend as long as a year with their mother. The raccoon has adapted easily to urban life, showing dexterity and ingenuity in opening doors, latches, and garbage can lids to get at food inside.

Ss

Sockeye Salmon
two males, one female

Salmon lay and fertilize their eggs in the same freshwater spawning grounds where they themselves originated. After the eggs hatch, the young salmon spend one to three years in fresh water before swimming to the sea, where they remain for several more years. When the time comes for them to make their return journey to the breeding streams, sockeye salmon change color from silvery blue-green to red, and their heads turn green. The male grows a hump on its back and its jaws enlarge. Both males and females swim vast distances—battling currents, jumping up waterfalls, and evading natural enemies such as grizzly bears—to reach the spawning grounds where the cycle begins anew.

Tt

Snapping Turtle
with minnows and brook trout

The snapping turtle, which lives in ponds, marshes, rivers, and lakes, has a long, flexible neck and sharp, powerful jaws that help it catch food. It eats fish, frogs, small mammals, waterfowl, and plants, and is also a good scavenger. Although the snapping turtle can be aggressive on land where it is vulnerable to attack, in its water habitat it is usually shy and unthreatening to humans.

Uu

Underground
with a meadowlark, earthworm, shrew chasing beetle, ants, larva, millipede, cottontail rabbits, field mice

Many creatures spend at least part of their lives underground. Earthworms tunnel constantly, passing large quantities of earth through their bodies, digesting only the dead plant material they need. The shrew digs for insects, its favorite food. Ant colonies build networks of tunnels joined to storerooms and nurseries. Other insects spend either their larval stage (some eating tender root tips) or pupal stage underground. Some mammals, such as mice, dig burrows where they store food, nest, and sleep, protected from above-ground enemies. The cottontail, instead of digging for itself, takes over another animal's abandoned burrow to nest in.

Vv

Meadow Vole
with a fox, hare, and red-tailed hawk

Meadow voles live in fields, eating seeds and vegetation. They are fast breeders, producing large litters, which mature quickly. Unchecked, a single pair of voles can have 200 descendants in a year. Some years are called "vole years" when their population sky-rockets, attracting many predators such as hawks, owls, and foxes. To make their movement from place to place almost invisible from above, voles make covered runways—in the summer they trample grass and eat away only the lower stems of plants along their routes, and in the winter they dig tunnels through the snow.

Ww

Whooping Crane
with a monarch butterfly, dragonfly, and turtle

Whooping cranes have a remarkable courtship dance, which few people have opportunity to witness because this bird is so rare. In the early 20th century, hunting and the destruction of its habitat decimated the species, and by the 1960s there were less than twenty left worldwide. Fortunately, with help, their numbers are currently climbing, and more whoopers complete the southerly migration to their wintering grounds each year. This majestic bird has a very long, coiled trachea, which enables it to make a loud trumpet call that carries across vast distances.

Xx

X-ray of Triceratops
with a Stegosaurus, Tyrannosaurus, Hadrosaurs hatching, Sauropods grazing

During the Mesozoic era, 225 to 65 million years ago, dinosaurs were the dominant animals on Earth. These reptiles came in all different sizes, some tiny, others 30 m (100 ft.) long. Many dinosaurs, such as the Stegosaurs, Triceratops, Sauropods, and Hadrosaurs, were plant-eaters, while others, such as the Tyrannosaurs, were meat-eaters. The dinosaurs died out 65 million years ago. Many scientists believe this was due to a climate change the dinosaurs could not adjust to.

Yy

Yellowjacket Wasp
with a garden spider and barn swallows

Colonies of yellowjackets, a common type of wasp, are primarily made up of egg-laying queens and female workers. Late in the season a few males arrive to fertilize young queens who, unlike the others, hibernate over winter. In the spring, the young queens build "starter" nests with "wasp paper" (chewed-up wood bits mixed with saliva), which their offspring will complete over the summer. By early fall, the nest may contain several thousand cells and two thousand wasps, all of whom will die except for a few select young queens.

Zz

Zoo
full of the animals you met in these pages

A zoo is a place of discovery, where animals are exhibited for people to view them. It is also a place where scientists can study animals up close, and conservationists who work to protect animals can learn what the animals need in order to survive in the wild. Zoos can't hope to save all endangered species, but they do what they can to protect wild animals from around the world and their wild homes.

123 Nature Notes

1
One Panda
in a bamboo forest

The giant panda, one of the world's rarest animals, is a native of China. Although bearlike, the panda may be related to the raccoon. It lives in high, mist-shrouded forests where bamboo, its favorite food, grows. A giant panda must eat huge quantities of bamboo every day to survive, and has even developed an extra "thumb" on its forepaws to help it grasp the stems. A newborn panda, pink and barely as large as a hamster, is carried in its mother's arms constantly for its first few weeks. The panda cub stays with its mother, growing and learning, until it is a year and a half old.

2
Two Giraffes
on the African savannah

The giraffe, at three times the height of a man, is the tallest creature on Earth. Tough hairs on its lips and a rubbery saliva coating its long, agile tongue make it possible for the giraffe to strip off and eat not only the leaves of such trees as the acacia, but also the twigs, branches, and thorns. Because its head is held so high, the giraffe can see much farther than zebras, wildebeests, ostriches, and baboons, who depend on this graceful animal for danger signals when predators such as lions approach.

3
Three Starfish
in a tide pool

The starfish or seastar, found in oceans around the world, belongs to a spiny-skinned family of animals called the echinoderms. A starfish can have five, ten, even fifty arms (always in multiples of five), which are symmetrically arranged around the central disk where its mouth is found. Each arm has two rows of tube feet, which the starfish uses to breathe, move, and gather food. Although it has neither head nor brain, a starfish possesses the amazing power of regeneration; a single arm with only a bit of the central disk can grow into a complete animal within a year.

4
Four Parrots
in a rainforest

The scarlet macaw, found in South American rainforests, is one of the largest parrots in the world. The macaw has two toes pointing frontwards and two backwards, an arrangement ideally suited to clambering in trees and grasping the fruit and seeds that make up its diet. It is an extremely noisy bird, raucously yelping and screeching especially in flight. The macaw, like other parrots, is an excellent mimic, and can imitate a wide range of sounds. Most macaws mate for life and nest in holes high in trees.

5
Five Tigers
in an Indian jungle

The dominant wildcat in Southeast Asia, the tiger makes its home in a variety of habitats ranging from mountain forests to lowland thickets. Tiger cubs are born blind and helpless. For two years they stay close to their mother, learning from her, and through rough-and-tumble play, the skills they will need to hunt and survive on their own. Because of hunting and the destruction of its habitat by humans, the tiger population has declined sharply over the last 100 years. Recent establishment of reserves and protective status for this majestic cat has already helped its numbers increase.

6
Six Crocodiles
on the banks of the Nile

When a female Nile crocodile is about ten years old, she lays her first clutch of eggs, burying them deep in sand beside water. When she hears croaking sounds, after nearly three months of guarding the nest, she digs up the eggs. The mother may help some of the tiny crocodiles hatch by gently rolling the eggs in her mouth to crack the shells. As they grow, crocodiles feed on larger and larger prey, quickly moving from insects to fish, rodents, and birds. Competition with humans for its habitat and food has made the Nile crocodile an endangered species.

7
Seven Monkeys
in the mountains of Japan

Snow monkeys, a rare type of Japanese macaque, live in the mountains of Japan. Some of these monkeys live farther north than any other primate except humans. To protect themselves during the long, cold winters, snow monkeys grow fluffy coats and huddle together for warmth. One group has even discovered that they can warm themselves by bathing in the local hot springs. When other food is scarce, snow monkeys survive on the inner bark of trees no other monkey would consider food.

8
Eight Camels
in the Sahara Desert

The one-humped Arabian camel is closely related to the two-humped Bactrian camel of Asia and to the llamas and alpacas of South America. Supremely adapted for desert life, the camel has a short, woolly coat to insulate against the sun's heat, long eyelashes and nostril flaps to keep out blowing sand, broad, padded feet to make walking on sand easier, and the ability to go for several months without drinking water. Its height even assures that its head is held just above the level of swirling sand during desert storms. The camel's hump is not used for water storage but holds fat, acting as a reserve source of energy when food is unavailable.

9
Nine Sparrows
outside a kitchen window

The familiar, cocky house sparrow, native to Eurasia and North Africa, now inhabits cities, towns, and farmland all over the world. All house sparrows in North America are descendants of a small number released in New York City in 1850. They quickly spread, eating insects and seeds and sometimes damaging crops as they competed with native species for food. The house sparrow usually has three broods of young a year, and nests almost anywhere—in gutters and ventilation holes, on streetlamps and signs, and sometimes in trees.

10
Ten Mountain Goats
on the slopes of the Rockies

Despite its name and appearance, the Rocky Mountain goat is really a mountain antelope. It inhabits craggy, remote slopes of the Rockies, far above the haunts of most of its natural enemies such as wolves, grizzly bears, and cougars. It is surefooted and moves deliberately, easily climbing cliffs, balancing on narrow ledges, and jumping as much as 3 m (10 ft.) from one rock to another. A mountain goat kid is playful but doesn't venture far from its mother. It seeks shelter under her during bad weather or when danger, such as a passing golden eagle, threatens.

11
Eleven Elephants
on the African plains

The African elephant is the largest land animal on Earth. Its huge ears are much larger than those of its cousin, the Asiatic elephant. An elongated upper lip and nose combine to form its trunk, which is so sensitive it can pick up a single blade of grass. With its trunk, the elephant can also suck water up to squirt into its mouth or shower over its head and back. When a female elephant is ready to give birth, the other cows gather around to help. The calf is born covered with hair, which it loses as it grows.

12
Twelve Ants
on a sidewalk

The ant, a usually wingless insect, is found around the world. An ant colony is begun by a single queen who lays a small number of eggs. When the eggs hatch, the queen feeds the larvae until they reach maturity. These adult workers are all female. They take over the business of the colony, digging tunnels and storerooms, tending eggs, feeding larvae, searching for food and protecting the nest, leaving the queen free for a life of laying eggs. After a few years the colony may contain hundreds of ants. At this time the queen produces a winged group of males and queens. These ants fly from the nest and the young queens establish new colonies.

13

Thirteen Whales
in Arctic waters

The beluga or white whale is sometimes called the sea canary because of its "singing." Through air passages in its rounded forehead, or melon, it produces a wide variety of whistles, ticks, bell-like tones, squeals, chirps, and sounds similar to those made by children playing in the distance. The beluga, a predominantly Arctic animal, is a small whale rarely exceeding 4.5 m (15 ft.) in length. The bluish- or brownish-gray calves become lighter as they age, turning completely white by the time they are five or six years old. Belugas feed in small herds on marine animals such as shrimp, fish, squid, and snails.

14

Fourteen Lemurs
on a Madagascan forest floor

Ring-tailed lemurs, related to monkeys and apes, are native only to Madagascar, an island off the southeast coast of Africa. The ring-tail lives in troops of five to twenty animals headed by one or more older females who defend their territory against intruders. They are active during the day, sunbathing, grooming one another, wandering about with their tails in the air, and leaping from tree to tree eating fruit, seeds, leaves, and bark. A newborn ring-tail is carried in its mother's arms for a month before it is strong enough to cling to her back as she moves about. Ring-tails and other lemurs are threatened by

the destruction of their rainforest home.

15

Fifteen Kangaroos
in the Australian outback

The red kangaroo, found only in Australia, is a marsupial, an animal with a pouch for carrying its offspring. A newborn kangaroo, the size of a bean, "swims" arm over arm through its mother's fur until it reaches her pouch where it nurses for six months. The joey first leaves the pouch when it is seven-and-a-half months old, but it returns frequently, tumbling in headfirst at any sign of danger, until it is too large to fit. The red kangaroo is an excellent two-footed jumper and, using its tail for balance, can leap 10 m (33 ft.).

16

Sixteen Crabs
on a sandy beach

The small, sideways-walking fiddler crab lives on sandy and muddy shores around the world. One of the male's two claws is much larger than the other. He uses this claw to signal or for ritual combat when protecting his tiny territory. Each crab digs a hole to hide in when the tide comes in, plugging it with mud so that there is just enough air to breathe until the tide goes out again.

17

Seventeen Tortoises
on the Galapagos Islands

The giant tortoise of the Galapagos Islands can weigh as much as 275 kg (600 lb.) and is probably a descendent of South American tortoises that floated on logs or debris to the islands thousands of years ago. Because it is a cold-blooded reptile, the Galapagos tortoise settles down to sleep in shallow, tepid rainwater pools to keep warm during the night. Instead of teeth, it has sharp-edged jaws

for nipping off the grasses, berries, and cacti that make up its diet.

18

Eighteen Prairie Dogs
on the North American plains

Prairie dogs live in towns composed of many coteries, or small family groups, each with its own observation mounds and network of underground tunnels, listening posts, storerooms, rooms for eliminating waste, and nest chambers. Using different barks, this rodent defends its territory, warning against danger such as the approach of a coyote, or gives the all-clear signal when it is safe for others to come out again. In the late spring, young prairie dogs leave their grass-lined nests to explore the world above ground where they eat grasses, roots, and seeds, and take part in social activities, such as kissing, grooming, playing, wrestling, and basking in the sun.

19

Nineteen Walruses
on an Arctic ice floe

The walrus, an Arctic mammal closely related to sea lions and seals, lives and travels in large herds. This huge animal, weighing an average of one ton, is protected from the cold by a layer of oily blubber up to 15 cm (6 in.) thick. The walrus uses its ivory tusks, which are overgrown canine teeth, for jousting or hoisting its massive bulk up onto ice floes. It finds mussels in the dark depths of the icy waters with its thick mustache of long, stiff whiskers, and feeds for up to two days at a time before lounging for another two on land. A mother walrus teaches her single offspring to swim by carrying it piggyback or holding it between her fore-flippers as she swims.

20

Twenty Tropical Fish
on a coral reef

A dazzling variety of fish are found on coral reefs, which are made up of the stony skeletons of billions of coral polyps. Most reef fish are territorial, and defend their food, hiding places, egg-laying areas, and night-resting spots. Reef fish are found in a myriad of shapes, sizes, and colors: some eat algae while others are predators or scavengers. Pictured counter-clockwise from the top left are: yellow snapper, a queen angel fish, blue-headed wrasse, banded butterfly fish, a spotted trunk fish, damsel fish, a queen triggerfish, a trumpet fish, and a sea horse. Twenty redhinds are shown in the border.

25

Twenty-five Butterflies
resting in a tree

The North American monarch butterfly can be seen congregating in large numbers in the fall. Incredibly, these delicate-winged insects migrate several thousand kilometres (miles) south to their wintering grounds, some as far as Mexico. There they hibernate in the same large groups before returning north in the spring to lay their eggs. The eggs hatch into tiny caterpillars with huge appetites. The caterpillars eat and grow until they are large enough to pupate. When the adult butterfly finally emerges from its chrysalis, it has enough fat stored in its body to give it energy for the long flight south.

50

Fifty Flamingos
in shallow waters

Huge flocks of pink flamingos are found in a wide range of tropical and warm temperate areas around the world. These flocks, sometimes numbering a million or

more, spend most of their lives wading in shallow alkaline lakes. They hold their curiously shaped bills upside down in the water to filter out algae and small marine animals for food. Because the areas surrounding salt and soda lakes are often barren, flamingos have few predators. Females lay a single egg in a mud-mound nest, protected from flooding and heat. Both parents produce milk, which they feed to their fluffy gray young.

100

One Hundred Penguins
in the Antarctic

The emperor penguin is flightless and stands an amazing 1.2 m (4 ft.) tall. Although clumsy on land, it is the most expert of all swimming birds, as agile while chasing squid underwater as a fish. The emperor lives in rookeries of up to a million birds and lays its single egg in the dark, cold Antarctic winter. For two months the male holds the egg on top of his feet, keeping it warm with a fold of skin on his belly. He does not eat during this time. When the chicks hatch, the females return to relieve the males and feed the chicks their first meal.

1000

One Thousand Tadpoles
in a pond

In the spring, frogs and toads lay hundreds of jelly-protected eggs in ponds. Each egg hatches into a larva or tiny tadpole, which soon develops gills for breathing, as well as eyes, a mouth, and a tail. Feeding on water-weeds, the growing tadpole gradually develops legs and lungs. Eventually the tail is absorbed into the body to provide food for the final metamorphosis of the tadpole into an adult amphibian, and the young frog or toad swims to land.

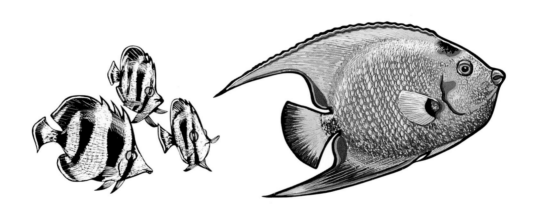